FINDING LOVE IN YOU, ME AND OTHER THINGS

Finding Love in You, Me and Other Things
by Rachita Baruah
Paperback Edition

First Published in 2024 in India by

Inkfeathers Publishing
Vivek Vihar, New Delhi 110095
www.inkfeathers.com

Content Curation Partner

ISBN 978-81-19483-37-2

FINDING LOVE IN YOU, ME AND OTHER THINGS

RACHITA BARUAH

INKFEATHERS PUBLISHING
www.inkfeathers.com

CONTENT CURATION PARTNER

mugafi

I am writing this book to find love in the other things.

"I would dedicate a page in my book just for you.
Mark my words."

∞ *and beyond*

Contents

CHAPTER 1

When Dhruv Met Rima

'Five minutes into the movie and then it had become unbearable. It was ten in the night, and he had to travel 600 kilometres on a video coach bus and join his bank the next morning. Speaking to the conductor was futile as the rest of the passengers were clapping to the explosive dialogues of Sunny Deol. Suddenly, someone from the back seat hollered at the conductor to play *Janmoni*, a musical Bihu video album. The conductor obliged. The boys in the back of the coach cheered at the suggestion while some girls blushed as the songs of *Jaanmoni* jostled up their euphoria of romance as the first lines goes as:

Sweetheart, please don't ask me how much love I have for you
It is as vast and deep as the ocean
You can't fathom the horizon of my love for you
It has the grandeur and magnitude of that of the sky
If I were a betelnut, I would have cut myself to show you my core
Or had I been a bird, I would have flown to meet you, my love

"I hope I had packed my headphones," Dhruv searched his backpack. He didn't have the energy to waste on romantic songs and took out the wiry pair, plugged them into his ears and played his favourite tracks on his mobile phone. He closed his eyes and his mind dissolved into darkness. He woke with a jolt when someone tapped on his shoulder. It was the bus conductor and, the bus was at its destination.

He forced his stiff body out of the bus with his suitcase and backpack. His head had a tinge of dizziness, and a glass of tea could waken up his spirits. He looked around, but there was no tea stall, only a few auto vans parked in a continuous line. The drivers gheraoed him and some even tried to grab his luggage. He pulled his luggage closer and boarded one of them and asked the driver, "Where is this van going"?

The driver, spitting out a mouthful of betel nut mixture, replied, "Depends on where the majority passengers are going, but for a hundred rupees it will go anywhere you say."

Dhruv handed him a fresh hundred rupee note and showed him the address.

"Wah dada. Fresh out of a bank," teased the driver as he pocketed the note and started the ignition of the Van.

"No dada, fresh into a bank if only you hurry and drive me to my destination. My first day in the bank starts in two hours and I don't want to be late," Dhruv synced with the driver.

"Are you new here?" inquired the driver.

"Yes, and I hope you are not Byomkesh Bakshi," an irritated Dhruv took out his headphones and plugged them in his ears and shut his eyes.

The driver drove for around five minutes, in silence, on the highway and then took a right turn and shifted to a narrow road. Dhruv opened his eyes, and his blurry eyes mistook it for a dream.

Had he landed on the set of a movie? The sun is peeking out to justify its presence by piercing its golden rays through an envelope of mist. Trees on either side forming an avenue were welcoming Dhruv with their benevolence. Beyond the trees were the dimly visible fields struggling with the mists to unveil themselves and afar stood the grandeur of the majestic mountains, perhaps snow-clad at this time of the year.

Too mesmerized but reluctant, Dhruv transported the entire scenery to his imaginary world that he created and adorned it with all the little good experiences he had in his life. This eased up his ordinary life, inundated with conflicts where he was just a mere spectator. He never had the courage to savour the sweet treats of a human life, as all he found was bitterness. His imaginary life bustled with all kinds of emotions, moments, and dreams, however, was devoid of one thing-people.

Soon the smooth pitched road turned coarse and bumpy with potholes. The Van Driver was quick to comment, "All Government Road Development Schemes ends here. In ten minutes, we would reach your destination, Jipran village."

He stood in front of a poorly plastered house with a rusty tin roof. The walls were once upon a time coloured with the cheapest quality distemper and the exact colour of the walls could not be determined as nature had adorned them with her own colours. Leaking of rain waters had discoloured the wall in patches and the sunshine had dimmed the brightness of either a cheap shade of blue or green. The windows had iron rods fitted to decayed wooden frames, and a single door guarded the scrawny structure. A big storm or a stout kick could assist in pervading the door of the sole bank in Jipran which guarded the money and dreams of the nearby population. A yellow painted sign board hung just above the door with the words 'Gramin Bank' written in green. He walked inside.

"Can I get some tea, with milk and sugar and please make it

strong," Dhruv requested Etuwa, the caretaker cum cook cum 'you say it-I do it for some consideration' man of the Bank.

"In the morning you get only black tea as instructed by Rima Madam, but for five rupees, I can arrange," Etuwa said while dusting the tables.

"Alright. Take these 50 rupees and violate some instructions of your Rima Madam.'

The room was abuzz with people. The Cashier Arun was quick with the currency and customers always surrounded him disregarding his advice of forming a queue. Two more staffs, Nabin and Lozen attended the customers, majority of them demanded to know their financial status as per the bank records. Rima was sitting in front of Dhruv. She wore a mustard-coloured hand-woven *Mekhala Sador* (traditional ensemble of two-piece garment woven out of cotton or silk in varied colours and motifs) with Night Jasmine motifs in red and white. A sweater in fawn colour matched the ensemble. She looked simple yet graceful. Her beige skin had no trace of makeup, and her eyes exuded warmth.

"So what are the directives I need to follow as per your diktats," Dhruv inquired with a smile.

"I didn't get you. Have I done anything wrong?" asked a perplexed Rima.

"I hate black tea,"

"Then don't drink, instead try warm water,"

"But I need tea to charge up myself and it is so cold here. A sweater is not enough to counter this cold," Dhruv had put on a checked blue and white sweater with black trousers.

"It's so cold here and rains incessantly that you will need a cup of tea every thirty minutes, so better forgo milk tea and switch to healthier options."

"Are you my mom," Dhruv instantly regretted saying this.

4

"No, your grandmom and call me if any real issue arises," Rima retorted and went back to her own seat.

"Krishna Prabhu Officer Saab. May I have a seat?" asked a man who seemed to be in his fifties.

Dhruv folded his hands in a Namaste and gestured the man to seat and asked, "How may I help you?"

The man asked his assistant to wipe the chair. His assistant took out his kerchief from his pocket and wiped the chair to his satisfaction. The man took the seat. He wore a pair of starched dhoti kurta made of superior quality cotton. It was spotless and freshly ironed.

"You or your miserable bank do not have the stature to help me, but I can obviously help you," smirked the man with a devilish laughter. His rotund belly laughed along with him and so did his dangling rosy cheeks.

"Sir, thank you for your concern, but I need nothing as of now. Namaste," Dhruv folded his hands again.

"Ah, I just came to introduce myself, as you are new. We will meet again and gradually be friends. Call me Maggan and if you wish to visit me, just ask anybody here. Krishna Prabhu." Maggan rose from his seat and left. His assistant followed him.

Dhruv was consumed by fatigue because of his overnight journey. His headache hadn't marred besides, he had to deal with so many people on the first day itself, some simple whilst others complex. He was leading a carefree life until the previous day. In his six months of intensive training, he enjoyed the lectures and assignments. Even the practical trainings were fun, but he soon realised that real work would be poles apart. He is unsure about this job or of any decisions he had made in his life. Everything is just a medium of escapism from his previous attachments, and he had trapped himself in this cycle of escapism.

"Sir, tea." Etuwa kept a mid-sized steel tumbler on his table. He had a small tiffin box in his hand. Handing it over to Dhruv he said, "Rima madam had made some rice cakes and told me to give you this box. I have brewed the best tea in pure milk, as per her instruction."

That was the only thing he desired at that time.

The Bank had arranged Dhruv's accommodation in advance. It was a part house and Etuwa would cook him dinner. It was a single, spacious room. The walls wept in morose blue. Even non-living identities desire some cheerful colours. A rustic wooden bed that creaked without grace when sat on, some mattresses, two blankets, a pillow, a set of table chair made of unburnished wooden planks and a garish brown almirah furnished the room. The furniture displayed inferior craftsmanship, but wall mirror attached in the wall intrigued Dhruv. The teak wood frame of the mirror was a misfit in such a modest set up. He looked out of the window. The silvery mist enhanced the beauty of the moon. Being a city boy, he craved to experience the beauty of a night full of shining stars. He zipped his jacket and went outside to fulfil his enduring desire.

The firewood warmed up the entire compound. The air smelt of mists, night jasmines and burnt twigs. Dhruv saw the silhouette of his house owner, Padma, near the fire. He went closer to the fire for a courtesy meet with Padma. She was tending the fire and covered herself in a dark woollen shawl in this chilly weather.

"Did u have your dinner, aunty"? asked Dhruv in the most courteous way possible.

She turned around and Dhruv gave an incredulous stare.

"You here," Dhruv couldn't comprehend if he was happy or indifferent to see an acquaintance of just one day in an unknown place.

"Yes. I have decided to follow you," said Rima in a jovial mood.

"No, I am really astonished to see you here. Do you know Padma Aunty?"

"Well yes. I live here,"

"O, she must be your mother then."

"Yes, but with a difficult extension…mother-in-law."

Chapter 2

When Dhruv Met Rima in Her Incognito Mode

On weekends, Rima would wander in the nearby wildlife rainforest which had captivated her imaginative mind since childhood. She would trail the paths of elephants or leopards and capture the paw prints on her mobile camera. She had a penchant for wildlife and loved interacting with squirrels or the capped langur in their own gibberish language. She was acquainted with all the paths and trails of the forest, but never ventured beyond the restricted areas.

There was an eerie kind of aura that chills you up to the bones. The towering trees hugged each other in affability, forming a dense canopy. Mellow rays of the sweet sun were touching the ground through a maze of green and dreamy silvery mist. The branches swayed to the synchronous rhythm of the January winds. Rima climbed up the machan. Despite being careful not to disturb the tranquillity of the forest, the bamboo stairs creaked at each step. A male Austen's brown hornbill perched on a branch seemed oblivious to the ways of the world. It had no inkling that Rima was waiting for weeks to capture a perfect moment of the species.

Rima took out her phone from her bag and cleaned its lenses. She set her camera focus on the Austen's brown hornbill and tapped the screen to lock the focus. With a steady hand, as she clicked on the shutter button, she felt a touch on her back.

"You?" Rima shrieked and lunged a few steps in fright.

"What are you doing here, and I suppose you are alone?" Dhruv's eye widened and also, he was a little nervous catching her off-guard in a secluded place.

"I was born here. This forest is my neighbourhood and I love being here and most importantly alone," Rima frowned.

"And what are you exactly doing as this seems so interesting to me?"

"Shooting,"

"Ah…don't you know shooting is illegal and unkind too,"

"But I am sort of unkind and love doing illegal things."

"Just like you denied me a cup of milk tea in my extreme urgency."

"Yes, but I offered you my destined piece of rice cake."

"So we are bound by destinies now if I go with your word."

"It's late. We should move from this place" Rima felt a flutter in her stomach and her mind raced for an apt reply.

The shanty tea shack was a temporary set up near the rainforest main gate. Glass jars containing locally made rice cakes, biscuits and savoury mixtures had been arranged in a line on a wooden shelf. Smell of cardamom and ginger tea filled up the shack. Gust of cold winds made the place even colder. Dhruv and Rima sat on seats made of tree trunks. The tea shop owner had served them cups of steamy milk tea and rice cakes on leaf plates. It was afternoon, and both were hungry. The much-needed food to fuel their engines to engage in further banters. Slurping on hot teas and munching on rice cakes, Rima pointed out to an empty seat in front of them, "Can you tell me what is the age of that wooden stump?"

"No, can you even? And I suppose you are a banker, not a botanist."

"I think you have skipped your class sixth science. If we cut a tree horizontally and count the dark rings, we know how old the tree is. The study of these rings is known as dendrochronology. So, this tree stump and all the seats in this shack are about eighty years old,"

"Wow, you are quite knowledgeable about forests. I have hardly been to one before."

"Hmm."

"Rima, can I ask you something? Actually, I want to ask two but..."

"Ask anything that I can answer," Rima said sheepishly.

"What were you doing in the machan?"

"Oh, that...I was trying to take a photograph of an Austen's brown hornbill. The name 'Austen's brown hornbill' honours Lieutenant-Colonel Henry Haversham Godwin-Austen. Have you ever heard his name?"

"Yes, of course. He was a British naturalist, geologist, and a great mountaineer. The Karakoram peak K2 in the Himalayas was at one time renamed Mount Godwin-Austen, in honour of its first surveyor."

"I am impressed. You have not skipped your Geography classes then." Rima chuckled.

"So photographing birds is your hobby, or you found that bird particularly cute?"

"Both. And I wish I had a professional camera just like the ones the tourists carry when they come here."

"It's not the medium but the person behind it who takes the good photograph," said Dhruv, raising an eyebrow like an aged philosopher.

"I wish your words were true."

"Can you show me the forest around?"

"The forest is perilous for strangers, and even more risky when I am there."

"I didn't get you,"

"You will know soon. Let's go from here before it is dark."

Chapter 3

Rima's Ordinary Life

Padma was working on a '*jotor*' (manual spinning wheel). She spun the cotton thread into the wheel with one hand while wrapping the thread into the spools with the other hand. The *jotor* was a rustic one made of wood and an old cycle wheel. She was somewhat apprehensive of the weaving task because of her aggrieving arthritis wearying her knees. She had low hopes on Rima for these types of household chores. Rima handed her a decent amount of money every month, cooked, cleaned, and brought groceries, but never took an interest in how a *jotor* works or how Padma wove a *gamusa* (woven cotton towel). She reminisced about the days when she collaborated with her own mother-in-law weaving out *gamusas*. The *gamusas* have a pristine white background, with vermillion red stripes on its three sides and red motifs on the fourth side towards its breadth. As a part of their culture, they presented *gamusas* to elders or loved ones on *Bihus* (festival of Assam) and other important occasions. And they wove colourful *mekhala sadors* with the exquisite detailing of animals, nature, and celestial beings as motifs. She lamented where the colours of their lives had vanished. Soon she was back to reality as her knee pain aggravated. He held on to a bamboo cane for support to stand-up. Her shoulders drooped forward and most of her weight had shifted to the stout bamboo cane. Rima rushed towards her to support her. She dropped most of the leafy greens that she had plucked from the unkempt garden in the backyard.

"I don't need your fake concern."

"Come ma, I will massage some hot mustard oil on your knees. You will feel better."

Padma melted a little. Rime took an earthen lamp, poured some mustard oil in it, and warmed it over another lit lamp. Then she took some camphor from the puja room and mixed it with the oil and crushed some basil leaves into it. She drizzled a little concoction on her palm and gently massaged Padma's knees. Padma was lying over a thin mattress on a wooden khat.

"We have got a new tenant. I think you know him as he works in the same bank as you."

"Yes ma. He is our new manager."

"I had decided long back to give out the part house in rent as the empty house constantly remind me of your father and Simanta."

"It is a wise decision ma,"

"Don't you miss Simanta,"

"I hardly knew him. I just met him for a day."

"Ouch…that hurts. Enough of your massage. You purposefully inflict pain on me."

"We should better consult a doctor soon."

Padma pulled a warm blanket over her. It was a sign for Rima to move away from there. She had heaps of chores to do. First, she went outside and picked up the leafy greens and then cooked a light dinner of rice, yellow lentils, and mashed potatoes with *khorisa* (fermented bamboo shoot pickle). She decided to wake Padma up at dinnertime and went to her room. She opened her steel almirah and took out a roll of manuscripts and unrolled them carefully. The pages were numbered and illustrated with rough sketches. She took out a blank page from there, drew margins using a wooden ruler and wrote in bold letters- Austen's brown hornbill.

Sometimes we give all our heart and soul to our dreams and suddenly some nonchalant thoughts invade it to steal some limelight. This same thing happened with Rima. All she could recall was the meeting with Dhruv after she had missed the chance of photographing the bird due to Dhruv's fault. What was the other question he wanted to know? Was she being too friendly with a stranger? Had she forgotten the day and its consequences when she met another stranger in the same rainforest a few years ago? She decided to restrict her meetings with him. Too much she was engrossed in his thoughts and a beep sound from her mobile phone distracted her attention. It was a text message from Dhruv, "Do you have anything to eat? Etuwa on leave."

"Will this boy give me some peace?" murmured Rima and she hurried towards the kitchen.

Dhruv was sitting on a cane stool near a kindling fire. The embers crackled and a shimmering bronze aura engulfed the surroundings.

"It is a beautiful night, isn't it?" Dhruv asked Rima as she walked towards him carrying a steel tiffin box. She warmed herself with a blue woollen shawl draped loosely over a cotton white *mekhala sador*. She neatly plaited her hair and had a grace in her walk. Her face shone in bright yellow and orange, just like the Palash flower shines in the sun's warmth.

"Please don't bother me again like this. I maybe your colleague at the office but here I have some respect", Rima's face glowed with a tinge of rage.

"Oh, that means I am an insignificant with no respectable value" Dhruv faked a sadness.

"I didn't mean that...And what is that?," Rima pointing towards a tall package near Dhruv.

"If you want to know, then help me to unpack this."

"What is it?"

"Bring a knife,"

"What?"

"Arey, bring a knife to cut the ropes to unpack it."

Rima rushed inside and brought a knife. Dhruv cut the ropes and revealed the Celestron Inspire 100AZ refractor telescope. Rima's anger dissolved as she saw a card attached to the package with 'Happy Birthday son' typed on it.

"Today is your birthday?"

"Don't fret about it. Just see the telescope. A perfect toy to kill time here" Dhruv's eyes gleamed for a moment and susurrated in the softest tone. "And also find myself."

"What did you just say" questioned an inquisitive Rima.

"Not today, Rima,"

"Rima" hollered a just wakened Padma.

"I need to rush now and a very happy birthday, Rima extended her right hand. "But I need the answer."

"Let us meet in the same place next weekend," and "Thanks", Dhruv gave her a mild handshake.

"Next weekend we have a village feast on the eve of *Magh Bihu* (a festival of Assam)"

Chapter 4

Festivities, Troubles and Rima's Turbulent Past

The air reeked of a blend of briny tang and rotten eggs. The bare feet felt slimy in sludge and the legs went numb in the icy cold water of the pond. The moon and the stars were invisible behind the dense fog. Dim yellow rays from battery operated torches and kerosene lamps barely showed each other's face but everyone knew the faces present there beamed with anticipation. The anticipation of catching the largest *'chital'* or *'borali'* fish for the night's feast. It was the eve of *bihu*, the day of the greatest feast of the year. The night of merrymaking and joy. Men and women teased each other with *bihu* songs and the young couples, married or unmarried, were undergoing a feeling of intense euphoria. Amidst all people, they endeavoured to steal a glance of their beloved. A gentle brush of fingers or an undeliberate eye contact ignited the passion of the couples, and they would sing with much ardour. The words of the songs were like a sign language to communicate their intense feelings.

Dhruv sat on a stone boulder near the community fishing pond. Being a city boy, he enjoyed the dawn of *'uruka'*. He was least interested in the fish haul however instantly sensed the fragrance of 'love' that wafted to the hearts of each soul present there. Was there someone who wouldn't fall in love in such an enchanted atmosphere? Dhruv's mind rushed to his childhood and then to his youth. He could not recollect any such face which fit his imagination of love. He had invariably attempted to keep a distance from people who invaded his personal space or forced associations with him. It had been a year; he last saw his dad or knew the whereabouts of his mother. He was unsure if he was happy not being with them, but at least he was at peace or presumed to be happy with no personal relationships or obligations. His mind wandered around the days his parents behaved as a normal family. His father, Ashim, was the best surgeon in Guwahati but as a family man, he faltered in his responsibilities. Dhruv was sent to boarding school at an early age, so he met his family rarely. His mother, Nitya, was an acclaimed painter often wandered in places in source of inspiration. Little did anyone know that she actually escaped loneliness. Ashim had bestowed on her all the things that could be bought with money, and all she desired was a little time and a spoonful of love. She enlivened the boring white canvasses with colours of both despair and hope. Admirers appreciated the harmony of hope and despair in her paintings but failed to comprehend the inference out of it. Ashim had often advised Nitya to commercialize her potential, but she was against the idea. Nitya had seen a lot of money in her life.

Soon it dawned. He saw Rima waking towards him along the trail of rays, brightening everything around him. For a moment, she looked like an angel descending from the clouds. Her smile towards him transported him to the other side of his mind, where he cherished all his fond memories. This was the one only time in his life, he wanted his both worlds to converge.

Rima came near him and handed him a jute bag.

"Maa had made some rice cakes. I thought you might be hungry."

Dipping a rice cake in tea, Dhruv said, "Oh Padma Aunty sent you here."

"No, actually I always come on Bihu mornings to meet my friends here."

"Will there be a feast tonight...," Dhruv's voice was overshadowed by the shouts of Maggan and his men.

Maggan stood on the rocky edges of the community fishing pond, with his hands on his waist, claiming his supremacy upon others. He signalled the head fisherman, Bhola, to come near him.

"Bhola, I think you had forgotten that last week, I had paid the village headman a hefty amount of money in lease of this pond for a period of three years and only I have the license to fish here."

"But Maggan *da* (brother), today is *Uruka* and we are not bound to your dealings with the head man. It is a community pond. Don't be so ruthless," pleaded a hapless Bhola.

"Let me be reasonable. My men will fish, and I will let you buy it from me at a reasonable price. Fresh and discounted. Rest fill will go to the town market for Bihu," smirked Maggan.

"So we now will have to buy our own fish," shouted the people who stopped all their fun, frolic and fishing and came to counter Maggan.

"Not your fish, but mine. My fish, my pond, and the entire vicinity of the pond. You guys pay or leave."

The dejected and angry villagers hurled abuses at Maggan. Womenfolk wept and cursed him. Maggan and his men, least caring about the jeering's, made their triumphant way towards the pond. They decided to forego fish this year and settle for meat in the feast.

Dhruv was amused but felt bad for the people. He had met numerous such unscrupulous people in his life. His city upbringing had given him such lessons from an early stage of life. His dad's home was inundated with fish and gifts during *bihu*, but there was not a soul to relish them. However, he felt pity on these simple people whose life and festivals revolved around the consumables harvested in their villages and *Bihu uruka* was a special day. Rima, too, shared with Dhruv her disappointment. She lamented people were not the same as they used to be. She rushed to take an account of the situation as her father too was among them.

Dhruv sensed an alarming botheration that Rima carried on herself. He was attracted towards her imperceptible vulnerability that she disguised as indifference. The wounds that she had tethered to heart, suppressed by her fine conditioning of societal norms, required healing instead of a ragged bandage, but at first, he needed to unfurl the bandage to gauge the depth of her lacerations.

The morning incident dampened the spirits of the people, but traditions were mightier than tragedies. Even during mourning, customs and beliefs took over grieving hearts and moist eyes. So, with low fervour, the festivities began. Over wood fire, black lentils simmered with taro stems. The aroma of duck cooked with aromatic ash gourd tantalized the nasal sensation, sending a signal of urgent hunger to the depressed minds. Shredded vegetables for stew and salad rested on banana leaves for the final assemblage. A few men stacked woods, bamboos, and hay to build a huge structure (*meji*) which was to be lighted the next day as a tradition while others prepared bowls and plates out of banana stems and leaves for the feast. Women still lamented about missing out on the fish delicacies and the atrocities of Maggan. Curbing on fishing might affect the collective economy of the village, resulting in loosening the strings of their scanty purses.

Dhruv sat on a seat of dried hay beside the warmth of the bonfire. He munched on savoury yam chips while his eyes scanned the length and breadth of the open field. She was nowhere to be seen. Then he saw Padma Aunty sitting among the women in a small wooden chair as seating on the floor intensified her knee pain.

Dhruv consciously realised that Rima had a past but felt an uneasiness, as his mind obligated an urgent desire to know everything about her. He stood up and went for a stroll. A few walks towards the open and he was obscured by dense fog. He felt his mind and body alike, completely lost in hazy dimness, with no emerging path to move further. His warm jacket failed to provide impactful insulation in this shivering cold, his icy hands felt numb, and an unclaimed drowsiness began swallowing him into a starved oblivion. Suddenly, out of nowhere, he felt warmth. His fingers entwined in a familiar touch and ears were soothing to the song of eternity. He heard his name, 'Dhruv' intoned with the synchronism of his heartbeat. He opened his eyes to another dream, Rima, right in front of him.

"Dhruv, you will catch a cold. Take this," Rima handed Dhruv a warm shawl.

Dhruv was now awake with a tinge of shyness and a smile. Were his both worlds coinciding in reality or was it a dream? He pinched himself.

"I want to know everything about you," Dhruv said with no introductory tidings.

"Everything means? Will you interview me?"

"Do you find funny in everything I tell you?"

"I find my life funny. To be honest, everyone here knows everything about me, but they don't know me" Rima sounded serious this time.

"So I want to know you, Rima" Dhruv brushed her index finger. Rima, with no emotion in her face, unfolded her life in front of Dhruv.

Rima's parents desired a male child and God blessed them with one when Rima turned ten. Before Ranjan was born, Rima bore the brunt of being the unwanted child and later her presence in their lives was entirely ignored. She was granted her share of basic needs and education, which earned her a decent job in the Bank. However, since childhood, there was not a soul with whom she could share her feelings, albeit good ones, as she never had disregard for anyone. She carried her dreams and desires in her soul, hoping to live them someday.

Rima was not a trained photographer, but with her basic mobile phone, she captured decent photographs of wild birds, hoping to add a visual treat in a compendium of wild birds she was working on. Her loneliness of a thousand words made their way in the form of poems, musings, and scribblings on notebooks. The pages in her diaries were witnesses to days of her successes, failures, lonesomeness, tragedies, and faith. Her life had instilled so much faith and courage in herself that she stayed aloof most of the time. Her parents were all busy with her perfect sibling and other social obligations that they found the silence of Rima to be immaculate for an adolescent girl. They boasted of her simplicity and taciturnity in front of the whole village in the hope of finding a match for her and they were so true as marriage matches poured in streams. Who didn't want a reticent bride with a bank job? However, she dismissed all the proposals under the pretext of providing some financial respite to her family for some time longer.

On weekends, she silently observed the hornbills and documented them in poetic verse and rhythmic lines. She patiently waited in the *machan* for birds to arrive and pose for her. On some days, she runs to along them to gauge their flight style. On one such a day, she met Simanta, a reserved forest guard who knew his way around really well. He was armed with a rifle, and a knife for both defence and clearing away paths of the forest. He assured Rima with guidance for the day as he knew the exact spots where hornbills had been recently spotted. He navigated through narrow trails and tracks and took her to the exact location where she spotted exotic and rare hornbills with vibrant plumage. She lost track of time while being engrossed in her work. Soon it started raining heavily and without umbrellas, they took shelter under the Hollong trees. Soon it was pitch dark and Simanta suggested they take shelter in the forest rest house and leave for the village as soon as the rain stopped. Their phones had no network, so she could not inform her family.

Rima could feel leeches sucking the blood from her calf and ankle and nodded to the suggestion of Simanta. The rest house was nearby, and both took shelter there. The caretaker welcomed them reluctantly as it was against the norms but took it as an exception because of the torrential rain. Rima was anxious being trapped in a forest with two men, one of which is a resident of her village who she hardly knew. She gulped down a bowl of tepid vegetable soup in hunger and angst. She spent the entire night without a wink of sleep. The rain had subsided by dawn and Simanta decided to drop Rima at her home in his official jeep.

Simanta and Rima got the shocks of their lives when both their families accused them of staying overnight in the jungle. Some neighbours added fuel to the fire and Rima's father faked a heart attack and fainted. Simanta's mother Padma concluded she was willing to take Rima for her daughter-in-law. Padma always had an eye on Rima and her well-paying job. Rima's father regained consciousness in a jiffy and blessed the couple. Nobody paid attention to the resistance from Rima as all started preparations for the wedding to be held the same night.

After the ceremonies got over, Simanta caught a fever. He had been hospitalised in the local hospital but passed away after five days, as the hospital lacked modern equipments to diagnose his dengue. In these five days, Rima stayed in Simanta's house and never returned to her father's home. Her parents had cautioned her never to step on their threshold with her ill-omened feet. Her inauspicious shadow might befall on their beloved son and that they are lucky to get rid of her.

Padma and Rima had no issues to discuss but Padma never failed to disgrace her in every moment of their lives. Padma lost an able son, got a daughter-in-law disreputably and her reputation in the village society dimmed. Her only respite was the income of Rima, so she tried to subdue Rima tactfully. She had laid several restrictions on Rima to display her dominance over Rima. The fact everybody ignored was that Rima's marriage to Simanta had no connection with his death. The only linking event was the time; cruel and harsh, who played with the destinies of the unfortunates.

Nobody ever thought about the plight Rima went through all these days. She had been through harsh days earlier, but this incident shook her entire existence. For the first few days, she wondered why was she living such a despicable life. In her parents' house, she had already been labelled as an unwanted occupant all her life, but now in an unknown house with unknown people with a widow tag on her forehead; she had nothing more to lose. She decided to stand up for herself. Without faltering in her duties, she would go for her job as usual and live for her dreams, whether they would come true or not. She would remain indifferent to any event, misfortune, or people in her life.

Till the end of her story, Rima's facial expression remained the same, but Dhruv was almost in tears. He couldn't believe the girl who seemed so confident, calm and at times teased him endured the agony of a thousand battles. Each day of her life was alike a battlefield where she had to escape from constant strings of mockery, criticism, or miseries. The most unfortunate feeling for a little girl was being desirable by her parents and Rima had carried that feeling in her heart for so long till all her feelings vaporised like a camphor. All that was left was the residue of the camphor with its fragrance lingering around her.

The fragrance of camphor mixed with the hazy fog to create an enchanted aura encircling them and Dhruv became lost in her deep, dark eyes. He could remain in this state forever or he wanted the forever to freeze. Rima, in her darkest nightmare, would never let Dhruv suffer for her, so she called out his name to interrupt his trance.

"Dhruv, it is getting too cold. We should eat our dinner and leave for home. Ma must be waiting for me."

"Let us wait here for some more time Rima," Dhruv pleaded.

"No, people might see us talking here in seclusion and it's not good for you" Rima moved away from his towards the people eating and celebrating *uruka*, the feast.

Two people went to home on empty stomach but their hearts overflowing with emotions. Rima controlled hers, but Dhruv let his emotions run with no repression.

Life had forever mistreated Rima and volleyed misfortunes towards her beyond her capacity. Initially, she was hurt and shed tears to release her pain, but gradually she developed immunity against adversaries. People say time is a big healer but for Rima, time was also her biggest vaccine against life problems. With time, she became skilled in tempting those misfortunes to steer their path away and assimilate them with life. She barely had an emotional association with people, however, she had a caring heart and endearing nature. Her job and tending to her mother-in-law consumed most of her time and the little spare time she got, she immersed herself in nurturing her dreams.

Chapter 5

Workplace Connections

In their workplace, Rima assisted Dhruv in scrutinising loan proposals. Dhruv had expertise in finance and Rima in people. While Dhruv had his calculations based on past accounting records of people, Rima thrived on her skills of negotiation and instinctiveness.

Tarulata's, a woman in her thirties, had no financial records as she worked as a daily wage earner in a nearby tea-estate. She got her wages in cash on Saturdays and had to spend her entire money on her ailing husband. Since Bihu, she had been visiting the bank for some financial recourse.

"Sir, please find a way to help her. She is from my *basti,* and I had assured her some help," Etuwa pleaded Dhruv.

"I understand your concern for her, but this Bank pays me for sourcing loans but won't take a second to fire me if the loan is not repaid on time," Dhruv said with a tone of sympathy.

"She can mortgage her home if required. You should visit them once," Etuwa referred to her rickety hut in the basti. Even the tiny piece of land they thought to be their own belonged to the tea garden's owner.

Rima chimed in, "Dhruv, the least you can do is to visit them once and see if a loan can be possible, provided Tarulata repays the money on time. Besides, there is always a wage report available with the accountant of the tea garden."

Dhruv never took financial decisions for the bank based on his emotions, but he wanted to give Tarulata a chance. He could also show this visit as a field visit for loan sourcing.

"Rima, I have decided to visit Tarulata's home on your insistence and if you agree, we both can visit her and analyse her case," Dhruv suggested her apprehensively.

"When do we go" Rima took no time to reply.

"Tomorrow at 10 in the morning. Please inform her," Dhruv took even a lesser time.

The new bike parked in the bank premises was glazing in winter sun. Dhruv's father had couriered the bike in a truck, and he had to reluctantly accept the gift. Dhruv mounted on his new bike and patted gently on the rear seat, indicating Rima to sit behind him. She followed his instructions and sat behind him, clasping her bag tightly.

"You can hang the bag on your shoulders and clutch the handle beside you," Dhruv said to make her comfortable.

She adjusted accordingly and clutched the handle at the back with her left hand. She couldn't figure out where she would place her right hand. Discerning her confusion, he placed her right hand gently on his shoulders and carefully drove away.

The Basti of the tea garden labourers was a disorganized colony of thatched roof houses with walls made of jute rags and bamboo tatters. There were no proper paths to the houses as the houses were scattered in a haphazard manner. Dhruv and Rima had to get down from the bike as mounds of waste and garbage obstructed their way. They saw Tarulata from a distance and walked over sludge and mosquito infested water puddles to reach her. Putrid smell coming from the garbage dump and nullahs made them cover their nostrils with their hands. Tarulata rushed to reach them, and they exchanged pleasantries.

"It's in pitiable condition Sir," Tarulata felt nervous to expose her dire financial situation. It was a two roomed shanty and stunk of urine. On a cot, laid a man in rags and bones. "He is my husband, Mohan. Doctor *saab* had given up on him. They say *libersesis* (Liver cirrhosis), but I know he would be on his feet before holi."

Dhruv remembered his father, who charged a bomb from wealthy patients for such cases. Costly transplants and healthy diets could save such patients but even if he granted a loan of a lac or two, it would not suffice the medicine cost, let alone the actual treatment and here, a loan of ten thousand rupees was also out of question.

Tarulata cleared a small table and served two cups of milk teas and *marie* biscuits. Dhruv felt guilty as Tarulata had to arrange all these on their visit, from the meagre amount that she had saved for her husband's treatment. He felt even worse about not being able to help her with a loan. He could donate a few thousand rupees to her from his savings, but it wouldn't suffice her need.

Rima stood a little strong. She preferred to be practical as she understood that Mohan's recovery was not possible, but she could not dare to break it to Tarulata.

"Madam, please have some tea. I couldn't offer much," said Tarulata with folded hands.

"Thanks, but you should not have splurged your hard-earned money on us. We just came to meet you," Rima regretted inciting hope to Tarulata by going there.

"Is there any possibility?" Tarulata's heartbeat could be heard from a distance.

Knock knock…there was a loud knocking at the door.

"Ah, Manager babu, the saviour is here. Then why did you waste my precious time? Don't you know my time is money? By the time I take a breath, my money grows ten folds," Maggan exaggerated loudly to show them his dominance.

Tarulata, with folded hands, pleaded both the parties, "Just save my husband. I am ready to do anything for that."

"Aah, anything you said…means anything!," chuckled Maggan.

"Yes, Maggan, anything to save him," Tarulata was in tears.

"I know these scholarly bankers have neither intention nor competency to help you…but I can," Maggan thumped his chest in pride.

Dhruv and Rima looked at each other in bewilderment. They understood Maggan was into some mischief.

Tarulata bowed down to Maggan with folded hands. Maggan rubbed her back maliciously.

"Taru, you are still young and beautiful. What is the use of your beauty if there is no admirer? I have friends in the city who would bestow you with all your needs…before Maggan could finish his sentence, he received a hard slap on his face. Rima had heard enough against the modesty of Tarulata.

Tarulata pushing Maggan out of her house shouted, "Let him die, then. If the world is this bad, we don't want to live."

"Great, don't come crying to me later. These useless bankers are of no good for our people. They just work for the profit of their bank. If they give you even one rupee, I will change my name. Thanks for calling and insulting me," growled Maggan as he left.

Tarulata cried inconsolably in Rima's arms.

"We will find a way, come to the bank tomorrow," consoled Dhruv.

On their way back to the bike, Rima asked, "Would you really help her or just consoled her for the time being?"

"You think I am a fluke? You didn't see how Maggan tried to disgrace her modesty? Surely, I have taken a decision to propose her name for the post of cleaning staff in our staff. Head Office had sanctioned a post."

"I agree on helping her, but you have taken this decision non judiciously. Are you going to provide a job to everybody who seeks your help or is she the only deserving candidate for this job? There are numerous Tarulata's and Mohan."

Dhruv calmly looked at her and said, "Time decides for everyone. If this time is right, she would get the job. In our lifetime, on very carefully chosen occasions, we get the chance to genuinely help someone. I am neither an activist nor a good Samaritan, but if I am chosen for this altruism, I would definitely respect my good fortune."

"You are raised right," Rima blinked at him and gave out a beaming smile.

He started his bike and said, "Nobody had the time to raise me, let alone right."

The wind sunk the audibility, but Rima heard it loud and clear. Had she heard him, right? He had his parents living in the city and his father was a well-known doctor, but he rarely talked about them. Even on his birthday, he was hesitant to talk about his father and the gift he had sent. Would she ask him, or time will tell? She left the decision on time.

Chapter 6

Confessing Dhruv's Past

Padma had gone to the nearby town to consult an orthopaedic surgeon. Her younger sister, Jaya, lived there and had undertaken the responsibility to take Padma to the doctor provided Rima bore all the charges for treatment. Rima had handed Padma a few thousand rupees even before she asked for it. Rima made a silent agreement with her obligations more out of pity than duty. She loved an empty house where she nestled her dreams. She decorated the house as per her liking or peel an orange and bask in the sun. Someday she would cut open a pomelo, mix it with salt, green chilli and relish it on a banana leaf. She loved this isolation. In her childhood, she imagined herself to be a member of the 'Swiss Family Robinson' who were shipwrecked on an isolated island. People who loved isolation could conquer anything. They are least bothered about validation from others. They loved their own company, just like Rima.

It was a lovely Sunday and Rima wrote a beautiful article about bird sightings. Her book was nearing completion, but she was a little disappointed with the photographs. After printing, the resolutions were quite dim for a book, but she was happy that she could send it to a publisher. For a while, she thought of purchasing a high-resolution camera with her savings, but she negated the idea as she required the money for Padma's knee surgery.

Her mobile beeped.

"Come to the backyard." It was from Dhruv. She rushed to the backyard to see Dhruv installing his Celestron Inspire 100AZ refractor telescope.

"You missed your dad?" Rima asked.

"No. I missed myself."

"What?" Rima was bemused.

Dhruv beamed with an infectious smile.

Rima was happy that she could at least bring a smile to his face. The wintry nights are always enchanted with a heavenly aura. Chirping of crickets, scent of night jasmines, a dreamy sky and a chill in the weather could awaken the senses of any human.

Rima broke the silence between them and said in a dreamy voice, "We are born for one special moment and the rest of our lives, we prepare ourselves to encounter that moment and savour it for the rest of our lives." "Other than that, our lives are useless; doing all the mundane activities to fulfil our carnal and social obligations."

Dhruv looked at her. She was glowing in divine brightness.

He grieved, "I have never had a special moment in my life. I didn't have a divine seat in my parents' lap just like my namesake prince Dhruva didn't have. However, Prince Dhruva, son of King Uttanapada and Queen Suniti, has his regal position above the north pole of the earth, the Polaris, or the pole star."

"I want to know everything about you," Rima said the same way as Dhruv had said her earlier.

"Everything means? Will you interview me?" Dhruv smiled.

"Tell me about your life."

"I will reiterate your words that we are born for some cause or a special 'something' that defines our life. My parents were lucky to pursue their dreams to savour that special moment of their life however, they were not made for each other. If staying together distanced them from their own purpose of life, I tell they made a good decision in parting their ways."

"So, weren't your childhood affected by their decision?"

"I had food on my table, roof on my head and attended the best boarding school. What could I ask for more? My parents were not the bickering type. For a long time, my father didn't even realise that he had been ignoring his family in terms of giving us his time and affection. Money was always there."

"And your mother?"

"She loved her art no doubt, but actually it was an escape from her marital lonesomeness. She never received the attention she deserved. On days she would paint all night and day and on other days, she would be gone to some exhibition or attend some course in the Himalayas to hone her craft."

"To be honest, I loved my childhood as I had been in my company in both joy and grief. Our emotional state is defined not by the events but by how we react to those. You know, Rima, the best gift that we can give ourselves is freedom of choice."

"Freedom of choice?"

"Yes, freedom to choose what goes into our senses. You can be cordial to everyone but there should a choice what we feed our soul. It really lessens our sufferings."

"I understand you, but I sense you have boxed up your feelings so tight that you allow no one to pass through your filter."

"Do you even know me, Rima?"

"Yes, I can see emptiness in your soul. You have fed good vibes to your soul, but it craves love, not empathy. You have been too empathetic to yourself."

"But I had several girlfriends in my school and college days."

Rima could not control her laughter at hearing this.

"Sorry," Dhruv's eyes moistened.

"Don't be. You know I was married forcefully to a stranger for no faults of mine. Just imagine how much I hate the word 'love' and 'relationship.' Now show me some stars in your telescope," Rima hid her sentiments by lightening up the mood.

"Do we really need to suffer, Rima? I am so involved in my work and the things I like to do that I have stuffed my desires into a non-existential apathetic cocoon. I even do not have the keys to release them."

"Dhruv, what is that one thing that you desire in your life?," Rima came near him and showed him. The first rays of the sun peeking out through the mist.

Dhruv felt a chill, as if he was just exposed to the wintry morning. They had no sense of time as they talked throughout the night. For the first time, Dhruv had clarity in his mind. He was consciously aware of the question Rima had asked him.

"Rima, If I can open up my heart to someone without being judged and the other person can connect to my feelings, I would be the happiest person in the world. But again, I would not subject that person to conditions."

"Do you think our loved ones will mourn us once we die? Yes, maybe for a few days, but life will go on for others. Life always goes on. It is us who hold on to the past, neglect our present and anticipate happiness in the future. If there is such a thing called love, it is inside you. People will love you, but you need to feel the love inside you.," she tapped gently on his chest.

Deep in his heart, Dhruv was sure that he loved Rima, but he would not subject his love to names and conditions. He would let time test his unflinching newfound faith in love. He needed to know himself first.

"Let us be ready for work," Rima said and went inside.

Chapter 7

Adversities Bring People Close

Rima went from work to her home early as Padma could arrive anytime. Padma arrived in a van and Rima hurried to receive her in the gate. After paying the driver, Padma let a sigh.

"Maa, was the journey comfortable?"

"It would have been better if Simanta had been alive. He always went to the bus stop to pick me in his Jeep," Padma let a sigh again.

Rima kept silence. He preferred to be a mute with people around her.

"These boys...how fast they drive their motorcycles these days. Sunu had nearly an accident. He is always oh high these days," Padma thrashed her handbag on the floor.

"Sunu, Maggan's son? Did he behave badly with you?" Rima enquired.

"He almost dashed his motor bike on our van. By God's grace, the van driver steered away from him. He is arrogant, just like his father showing off his ill earned money, but what is the use telling you all this? Just boil some water. I need to bathe," Padma murmured something and went inside.

At the dinner table, Rima served yellow lentils, cauliflower curry and rice for Padma.

"What did the doctor say?" Rima asked.

"I require knee replacement surgery immediately. The doctor says some gel inside my knees had dried up," Padma touched her weak knees.

"How much money is required for that?" Rima needed the calculation.

"Almost two lakhs. Jaya has assured me to help me with the stay and hospital chores, but I can't ask money from her. I have no savings left except the meagre family pension and the rent."

"Don't worry, we will sort out something," Rima did some mental calculations.

"I am done with the dinner. Please give me a bag of hot water. In this cold, my aged bones shiver to the core." Saying this, Padma left for her room.

Rima had saved some money to buy a camera, but she felt Padma's need was bigger than her wants. Sometimes Rima wanted to escape from this forced relationship but change in distance would not guarantee peace of mind. Going to her parents' home was impossible. She had made plans of taking a transfer to some other place, but that too was not entertained by her employer. She made a truce with her existing condition for the time being. Being herself and listening to her inner voice made her life bearable. She sat in front of the mirror and analysed her reflection. Who was that person in the mirror? Rima or Simanta's widow? No, there was this soul who craved not for an identity but a meaningful life. Someone whose heartbeat for a reason, someone who could go sleepless nights for a purpose, and someone who could face the world for self-righteousness.

Rima dreamt of being a writer and started her journey by documenting wildlife series. She had never thought it as an alternate career but as a passion where she could write her heart out. Everyone in this world is ever ready to pounce on soft targets and dissect others' beliefs that do not resonate with themselves, but she was ready to take the chance. If none, but at least the universe would correspond to her desires and give her due happiness not in relative measure but in actual where she can walk with closed eyes and an open heart and if she falls, there will be a hand to hold her. And when she opens her eyes, she would see 'Dhruv'.

The thought of Dhruv transported her to the real world in front of her mirror. Her cheeks turned rosy, but she shunned her thoughts, relating them to be the lingering aftereffects of that night. She switched off the sleep and tried to sleep, but sleep was miles away from her.

Her phone beeped. It was Dhruv. He had asked her to meet him in the morning, an hour before office.

Dhruv was in front of the office. He had a frown on his forehead, as if in deep thoughts. Etuwa was standing beside him and along with them was Sunu, Maggan's son. Sunu barely stood upright and repeatedly collapsed in Etuwa's arm. Dhruv beckoned Rima, and she obliged.

"These guys are not up to good things," Etuwa said.

Rima saw merely Sunu, so Dhruv cleared her confusion about the phrase, 'these guys'. Sunu's father's ill earned wealth attracted the village youths towards him like fruit flies on rotten fruits. His fancy bike, shiny jackets and unlimited pocket money had earned him superfluous friends who got bored playing with mobiles and village belles. They decided to take the game to an edge, so they befriended some truck drivers who run their trucks through the highway adjacent to their village. The motive was to trade contraband drugs smuggled all the way from the bordering areas.

Trifling fun turned into obsession and later into addiction. The night before, Dhruv and Etuwa after dinner went for a stroll to find Sunu, Ranjan (Rima's brother) and Neel, a friend of Sunu, in inebriated condition in a makeshift tent erected in the rice field of Maggan. It was too late to find a doctor or inform their parents. So Dhruv decided to have a talk with them in the morning, in the presence of Rima. Neel fled in the morning and Ranjan hid behind the banyan tree when Rima came. He was ashamed that his sister was aware of his misdeeds.

"Ranjan, come out of the hiding. Let us go to the Friday market. Sunu, you too come. We all will have a nice breakfast before I commence my duty today. We can walk our way to the market," Rima said as lovingly as she could. She knew it was a hard task to counsel today's youth. Ranjan came out of his hiding, sheepishly. His eyes were red because of the last night's substance abuse. He seemed frail. Rima had raised her brother from the day of his birth, and his pitiable condition broke her heart. Nobody could control another's fate, but she felt guilty of her brother's condition. Even if she complained to her parents about Ranjan, they would just cry and blame their luck or, the most, they would send him to a rehab in the town. In her village, rehab meant mental hospital and the family would be subjected to mockery.

Dhruv walked ahead of them. Rima, Ranjan, and Sunu followed him to the breakfast eatery. Puri, bhaji and mango pickle had been served on steel plates with compartments. Sunu tried to sprinkle the clumpy salt from a plastic dispenser and got irritated when the cover fell onto his bhaji with the entire bottle of salt. Ranjan scanned the room as if it was his first visit. His gaze halted on the container of orange candy. Rima noticed him. She got up and walked towards the counter and returned with a handful of orange candies that were a part of their sweet childhood. She handed candies to both Ranjan and Sunu. Sunu pushed the candies aside and fiddled with the pepper dispenser this time.

Rima broke the silence among them. "Do anyone of you have a lighter?"

Ranjan and Sunu looked at each other's face. Ranjan felt a flutter in his stomach. He didn't have the audacity to smoke in front of his sister. The weight of the lighter in his pocket felt heavier than his entire weight. He shifted his attention to his uncut toenails. People cut and discard the long nails as if they are trash, but they belong to our body. Do we discard every unless stuff related to our body and relation? Ranjan feared Rima would throw him away from her life. He loved his sister and secretly admired her grit and perseverance. When she dealt with her misadventures alone, he could not protect her due to his selfish attitude. He sided with his parents to get her married for that obscure reason. He discerned that all the girls were just born to get married and settle down and saw no fault in Simanta. But after Simanta's death, he was trapped in guilt. The miseries of Rima haunted his conscience continuously. He was to appear in the board exam that year, but on the pretext of group study; he grouped up with Sunu and his gang for some cheap relief. He felt panacea trips were far better than guilt trips.

"Here it is," Sunu handed Rima the lighter that he had bought from the Friday market.

With a powerful motion of her thumb, Rima rolled the spark wheel down into the ignition button. A tiny stream of butane gas released, igniting a spark. She took a piece of stray paper and burnt it. Ranjan felt a relief with her action. His sister was just being playful. Next, she placed her index finger in the mild flame and felt a slow burn. In reflex, both Dhruv and Ranjan lunged to snatch the lighter away from her, but she didn't let the lighter go.

"Explain to me your action," she looked towards Ranjan.

"You could have got a burn," said Ranjan.

"And how does it matter to you," Rima narrowed her eyes.

"You are my sister, and I would have stopped anyone from doing it. I know it will hurt a person severely," Ranjan gathered a little courage.

"And you think, whatever you boys are doing will not hurt you", Rima held Ranjan's hand, "You can see the immediate reaction of my action as it gives the result instantaneously i.e. the burn but you cannot fathom the repercussions of your action, needless to say both physical and emotional."

Ranjan knew the repercussions, but he least cared about his health. He just wanted to destroy the monsters in his head, and it was going all fine until then. His eyes were now darted over a few lines written on a blackboard with white chalk. He was struggling with the words even when, they were written in English.

shraddhāvānllabhate jñānaṁ tat-paraḥ sanyatendriyaḥ

jñānaṁ labdhvā parāṁ śhāntim achireṇādhigachchhati

"I just need a little peace in my mind," Ranjan said in the most silent tone he could, but it was enough for everyone present there.

"Do you know the meaning of those?" asked his sister. Ranjan preferred silence.

She read out the lines fluently and looked towards Ranjan, "Attaining everlasting peace is in our hand albeit we need to trust and know what we are doing."

A hopeful spark ignited in Ranjan's mind, though he couldn't comprehend what she had said. Understanding his mind, she further said, "The tea shop owner daily writes a line of Bhagwat Gita on this blackboard. From my childhood, I had tried to interpret them. Various people give their own interpretations, but I try to find the significance of these lines in my life. Now for me, these lines give me hope. What lies is front of me is unknown, the paths treacherous.

I need to have faith in myself and the universe so that I can overcome whatever difficulties lie ahead of me. Belief that every problem can be resolved solves half of the problem. We need to find the right path and not wander into insignificant routes. This knowledge having faith in ourselves of choosing the right way or wrong way decides our life, our peace, and our happiness." After a short pause she continued, "Sometimes to know about a path, we need to walk a little distance to feel its vibes, but we can always return if the path leads to pain, both mental and physical. The choice is always ours."

Dhruv was stunned at Rima's words and knowledge. Now he could understand how she withstood all the turbulent storms of her life. He didn't say a word as that was a moment between the siblings which he had never experienced in his life. He was overflowing with multiple emotions; the most was sincere love for Rima.

Sunu got up from his seat. "You guys continue this moral science classes. I am bored but thanks for the breakfast" and left. He had a lot of money to solve all his problems in his life. Least he needed was a lecture from a woman.

Rima rose and indicated Dhruv to go to the bank. She would come after taking Sunu to home.

Rima and Sunu were late as Maggan and Ranjan were standing at their threshold talking to their parents.

"Ah, here comes Mrs. Branch Manager, saviour of all," sneered Maggan.

Rima shouted from a distance, "Why you are here?"

Maggan was waiting for this. "These two siblings are everywhere. Can't I even come to your home?"

"What do you mean, Maggan?" asked Jyoti, Rima's mother.

"Jyoti, you have birthed two warriors who threaten everyone who doesn't comply as per their wishes. Let me tell you. Ranjan forcefully took my son to the drugs seller, extorted money from him and tried to induce him into drugs. My son, Sunu, somehow escaped from their clutch but again nabbed by your daughter and her sidekick, the Bank Manager to extort some more money. These two love birds could be seen everywhere. Ask anyone if you refuse to believe." Maggan took a deep, satisfying breath.

Ranjan lunged towards Maggan, but Rima clasped his hand.

"Look, how a ruffian he is? He beats anyone who refuses his orders. We are leaving for the time being but if I see any of you near my child, I will put all of you behind the bars" Maggan poured some more oil in the flames and left.

Jyoti started to wail and beat her chest for birthing two monstrous offspring. One ate up her spouse and brought ill luck to the entire family and the other had plans to devour the whole village. Rima went to console her mother but was pushed back by her. Rima was already the bad influence on her brother. Maybe Ranjan did whatever that Maggan had just revealed on the behest of Rima.

How supportive couldn't a mother be for her own child? An outsider came and labelled allegations on her children and she couldn't even defend them. Such are the norms of our society? People backed by money and power could be right on both the sides of a coin. Or the mother is weak enough or blinded by societal conditions to disregard the legitimacy of the weaker party, even if they are her own identity. Jyoti was a probable front-runner in the rat race of society, falling to the intrigues of bearing a male child, measuring competencies of siblings, and unburdening her shoulders by marrying off her daughter under societal pressure. Today she would wail off her sins of birthing such offspring and parade her consolation trophy in front of everyone.

Rima's father, Hemo, desired a real heart attack to escape this situation. He had been an escapist all his life, but God had granted him with great health. All the people in this world honestly needed just a bit of courage, self-confidence and capacity to rationale thinking, which was lacking in Hemo. He favoured his children, particularly Ranjan, but he was not in a position to counter Maggan. Hemo too lamented in loud wails, cursing their parenting.

Jyoti dragged Ranjan to the inside. "Rima, we are ashamed of being your parents. We will look after Ranjan. Just get lost from our life before I convey your deeds to your mother-in-law. We have no more to give you. You have humiliated us enough."

Sunu gave a wicked smile, as left clutching to his father's hand, after placing all the blame upon Ranjan. His father caught him after he left the breakfast joint as news Maggan got hold of Neel, who had fled the scene earlier. Neel spilled partial facts when he was asked the whereabouts of Sunu, who didn't come home for two days. Maggan believed his son blindly and also had the power to shut anyone's mouth with money and power. Such is the power of wealth. It can buy morality and worldly happiness. It has got all the shortcuts to the hindrance paths of society. That day, money chose Maggan as the better parent.

Before leaving, Rima looked into the eyes of her brother. They conveyed her affection for him and her words "Attaining everlasting peace is in our hand, albeit we need to trust and know what we are doing."

Rima had no mood to work that day, but she was aware of her responsibilities. She reached late for work, but Dhruv knew everything. He urged her to take a day off, but, she refused, saying she was better off here than being at home. Maggan may had fuelled some fire in her mother in law's mind too and she was not ready at that time to absorb further humiliations. Stones also get washed off with regular friction and she was merely a human. She had to nurse her own wounds. Her despair sometimes turned into depression, but she had learnt the art of overcoming every situation. She knew she could fly away from her cage anytime, but she waited patiently for her people to open the doors of her cage and let her fly in the open without any obligations. She felt a little feverish, nonetheless she attended to customers as much as she could. It was not a part of escapism, but a measure to re-establish her sanctity.

"Tea," Dhruv placed a cup of tea in front of her. Rima was thankful to Dhruv for not inducing any heroism and interfering in such a sensitive matter. It required an act of solemn restraint as arguing could had enhance the situation in worse ways. Rima despised heating up situations unnecessarily, as every problem did have an amiable solution.

"Do you know Maggan's actual problem is me?"

"Not only you. He despises all the people working or who had worked in this bank. It takes away his monopoly in lending to the villagers. We had never cared for him as he is just a fizzled out wet firecracker. His explosive dialogues couldn't even scare a kid, let alone me. Just sometimes, his money made some horrendous jingling sounds to scare away the timid."

Dhruv burst into laughter. He was amused with the reference Rima made of Maggan and the people surrounding her. He had never seen such a girl, or rather a person. He so wanted to become a bit like her and gather the courage to take her away with him to a place where she could live peacefully. He really wished for that courage to convey his love for her, and he would sincerely work on that to win her heart. But for the time being, he is one of those 'timid'.

"How is your photography going on?," Dhruv changed the topic.

"Actually, I am working on an encyclopaedia containing article and photographs both local and migratory birds of the rainforest. I have nearly completed it, but I am not satisfied with the photographs. They are of inferior resolution and do not serve the purpose."

For the first time, Dhruv saw a hint of dejection on her face. He made up his mind to help her some way, but she was too humble to accept anything from others, but Dhruv was adamant. It was nearing evening and closing time of their Bank. Dhruv asked Rima if he would accompany her to home, but she declined. She was aware of the prevailing situation and didn't want Dhruv to be further embroiled in it.

It was a cold night and relations, had grown colder. Rima understood the subtlety of complex relations, but she could never ignore her responsibilities. She roasted a round brinjal in the hearth of embers. She knew brinjals cause arthritis to flare, but Padma insisted on having roasted brinjal mash and lentil fritters. Sometimes Padma behaved childishly to annoy Rima. In the village, Padma had no close ties except her rheumatoid arthritis pain, so she invited her pain occasionally. It was her strongest weapon to dominate Rima and get some more attention from her. She indulged in the gentle oil massages and the hot water bags provided by Rima. She loved to curse Rima on the pretext of cursing her pain and that brought relief to her pain both externally and internally. As a human, it was surprising that she didn't feel an iota of pity for Rima. Actually, it was more of jealousy rather than abhorrence. Rima had an air of clandestineness around her. Her calm and non-judgemental nature acts as a shield which is often visible to the people around her, and many are intimidated by it. Padma was desperate to keep Rima in her most submissive persona to dominate her. There are so many races going on in our life and everyone is hell bent on excelling, be it greed, recognition, or an upper hand in power. However, Rima was on an inimitable stratum of life. She floated effortlessly on the ebb and flow of life, matching to its rhythmic synchronization. She cared less about being a successful social animal by jumping on the same race rather, she desired to experience the vagaries of life. What is pleasure if you have not experienced any pain? All pleasure and no pain take away the feeling altogether; the feeling of being alive and kicking.

"Can't you be a little generous with the sugar? The *payash* is totally bland. If you have run out of money to buy sugar, tell me. I still have good intentions to feed both of us," Padma added some melted jaggery to the rice pudding.

"Doctor has advised you to consume less sugar, Ma."

"As if you care. At least let me die with some sweetness. From now onwards, restrict nothing in my food. I want to die a happy death. With these sore knees, I have no intention of living any longer. Who would donate lakhs of rupees for my knee operation?"

"You need not worry. I have saved some money. Your treatment will be done as per schedule. I will arrange two lakhs for your operation."

"Let us see. Who knows what is in the future? Meanwhile, give me some unsweetened *payesh*. I have added too much jaggery to this portion and discard the brinjal too. It is full of alkali and seeds."

Rima smiled at Padma's silliness. She had saved around two lakhs' rupees to buy a decent camera and for exigencies, but she would have to forgo her wish and postpone her project. However, she didn't lose heart, as she knew money was as capricious as life itself. And for her dreams, they would always remain attached to her, whatever the situation may be.

Rima's phone beeped.

"Not asleep yet. I can see your lights on."

Rima replied, "Go to sleep."

"Let us go to the rain forest tomorrow. We need a change."

"It's not safe for you."

"I don't want to be. Just need to spend time with a non-judgemental person."

"Alright. Goodnight," and she switched her phone off.

Chapter 8

Inner Voices

After time, nature is next best healer. The soothing contrast of greens, browns and the blue sky instils subtle good vibes in us. The tricky game of sun and shade while walking through the narrow paths beneath the trees awaken our visual senses. The pure air freshens our aura, and the ignites our natural instincts. The gentle touch of the breeze and sometimes the howling sounds of the strong winds made us feel awake and human drawn towards our inner voices. Listen to the voices. They are ethereal and show us the right directions. The direction to indulge in the oneness of body and soul: the heavenly bliss. We learn the most important lesson from these forests: humility and benevolence.

The nature has a great hand in shaping Rima's mind and character. She took more interest in nature than in people, so she learnt the veracious traits of life. While returning on a hot summer day from school, the rich kids and their parents with big black umbrellas had never shared some shade with her but the row of mighty trees on the roadside serves as a big umbrella to her and all other people irrespectively. One day, it rained heavily on the way to her home. She took shelter in the Bhole Baba temple, which was built just near the forest gate. She considered the temple as a part of the forest. The priest, Vishwanath alias Vishu Baba, was a benevolent man and Rima regarded him as a part of the forest as well. Often, she visited the Bhole Baba temple to pay her reverence to both Bhole Baba and Vishu Baba. Vishu Baba would give her a Prasad of fruits or dried *bundiyas* and enthralled her with stories of his visit to the Kumbha Mela or his penance in the freezing Himalayas. He would often conjure up some mythical characters and assimilate them in his stories to make them interesting.

He once gifted Rima a charm, sort of a pendent depicting a half-moon that Shiva adorns on his matted hair. She tied the pendant on a black thread and wore it every day of her life. It rooted her to the forest and kept on reminding her to be herself.

The roof of the temple was covered with moss and orange trumpet vine flowers. The structure looked surreal, godlike. Perhaps Bhole Baba had himself crafted this abode. It was a stone structure with damp orange walls. People of the vicinity often thronged there out of devotion or want. The 'want' ranged from health, wealth to offspring.

Rima and Dhruv sat in the small compound of the temple. It was devoid of people. Perhaps Bhole Baba had blessed every one of their wants. Dhruv's phone rang, and he excused himself for some time. Rima wandered around the temple that was familiar to her. She knew every inch of that area. Vishu baba was somewhere in Varanasi to learn some siddhis as far as she knew. He would return by Holi. Dhruv was gone for more than half an hour, leaving her alone. She felt a little petrified rather than annoyance as these forests also conceals some unknown dangers. Was she missing Dhruv? A separation of half an hour or more meant nothing to her, but they are in the forest. It contained a magical charm, where deepest secrets unearthed with a little tap.

Dhruv was back, and so was her smile.

"Sorry, I kept you waiting for so long," his face looked apologetic.

"It is absolutely ok. I too took a stroll around the temple. It holds so many childhood memories of mine, basically the good ones."

"And share some. I took want to experience the good things of life, especially of childhood," Dhruv's frowns clearly showed a displeasure.

"Do you want to share anything because before the phone call, you looked serene but now you are sporting a frown on your forehead."

"Actually, papa called. He is permanently shifting to London and wants to take me along."

"And did you oblige him?"

"No. I am extremely certain that he would be busier there, and I would just work in some MNC to live a soulless life. Besides, my mother is here."

"Do you visit your mom?"

"I had visited her last year in Darjeeling in one of her exhibitions. She eminently wanted me to stay with her, but she herself is a wanderer. How could I keep in pace with her? I would be with her when she requires a walking stick for support and a shoulder to rest her head. In my childhood, I missed her a lot, but now I am so proud of her. She didn't require the society to recognise her inner self. Few people on this earth tread on the path they create out of passion and their inner voice," Dhruv looked at Rima. She resembled his mother a lot. They both tread on the path created not by destiny but by their inner voice.

"Do you know where your mom is at present?"

"Yes. She is coming to a nearby town in the next month for an exhibition. I intend to visit her there."

"We both can visit her. I could actually feel her. She must have gone through a lot of inner turmoil to decide the paths of her life. And some regrets too. Pain is a more powerful binder than pleasure.

And the same pain binds us."

"And how is Ranjan? I have no hope from Sunu and his gang, but Ranjan is clearly lost. We need to show him the right path and bring him back to his studies."

"Dhruv, I think we should not meet outside of our workplace."

"Why?"

"I don't want your name to be tarnished."

"So, Maggan had stooped so low. But why do you worry about others? Let them say as they wish."

"Still…It might hamper your reputation."

"I just know that we are soul friends, and nothing can make us apart till death."

"O, wow, is it a vow…till death do us apart?"

"Sort of," Dhruv smiled.

"How can you be so sure that I too think in the same line as you," Rima smiled too.

"Your smile and your eyes. They say it all. The purity of our pain unites our souls."

"Till death do us apart and thereafter," Rima vowed.

"Forever."

"Let us go to the tea stall for some tea and leave before dark."

"Let's go."

Chapter 9

Overcoming Adversities: Bring People Closer

After a strenuous day at work, Dhruv was retiring for the night. He climbed on his clammy bed and pulled a warm blanket over him. It had been raining the whole day, and the weather is quite damp. He took out his antique leather-bound journal. Most of the pages have been marked by sticky little flags. He searched for the faded green one among the other worn-out butter-coloured flags and overturned to the page he was looking for. It is almost a sleep time ritual for him to read a few lines of his journal or scribble something on it. He read the poem 'Solitude or Loneliness?'

> *I metamorphose*
> *Into a poem on solitude and;*
> *You innocently pile me*
> *Into your manuscript of loneliness.*

He read a few more lines until sleep crept over his brooding eyes. He had a series of unlinked dreams until he heard a thud. He woke up gasping for some air. With a splitting headache, he scrabbled around his side desk with his fingers, trying to find the alarm and buzz it off. Dhruv could barely open my eyes. He was still in his sleep, with a trace of his dream playing in his head. He somehow crawled out of his bed and looked out of the window with a broken pane. It is still dark and raining. He drank some water from the plastic water bottle.

There were two more thuds followed by sharp knocks at his door. He opened the door to see a distraught Ranjan and beside him was Rima.

"Is everything alright?"

"I am sorry, Dhruv dada. Last night, Sunu and his gang lured me, and I followed them to the old school premise. It was empty and Sunu lighted some cannabis joints as refresher. I took a puff but felt uneasy. I decided I would not allow myself to inflict pain on my sister's name and feelings, so thought of running away from there. But it was too late, and no one would open the gate for me, so I decided to wait there till dawn and then return. I dozed off and when I woke up, I just saw Sunu. He was vomiting and his mouth was covered with froth. All others had run away observing his condition."

Rima took over. "Ranjan came to our house and called me to the gate. Dhruv, we need to help Sunu or else he might die."

Dhruv freshened in a minute and took out his bike. They went to the old school compound and found Sunu gasping for air. There would be no doctor in the village hospital, so Dhruv and Ranjan put Sunu between them on the bike and drove to the town hospital. Meanwhile, Rima went to Maggan's house to convey him the news.

Maggan's iron grilled gate was open. She rushed inside and pressed the calling bell. An irritated Maggan opened the door after she has pressed the bell continuously.

"You. Don't tell me you have come to ruin my morning by

arguing with me for that day's matter. I have no mood to talk to nitwits like you," shouted Maggan.

"I have no time to argue, but your son is in danger," and she narrated him the incident.

"Oh, you siblings will kill my child someday," cried Maggan.

"It is not the time to play the blame game but rescue Sunu. Let us go to the town hospital," Rima was irritated this time.

"Pori," shouted a distraught Maggan. His wife came hurriedly. "We need to reach the town hospital immediately," Maggan sat on his car. Driver Ramu was ready in a jiffy. Rima and Pori sat in the rear seat. Pori cried the whole way. Maggan dialled some numbers and took the information. He had people to apprise him about his vicinity.

They reached the hospital. Sunu was taken to the emergency ward where doctors doing the night duty had already started his treatment. The others waited outside until one doctor came out.

"How is he, doctor? Please treat him well. He is my only child. There is no death of money for him," Maggan fumbled while speaking.

"He is still in critical condition. No money can assure his life but only good wishes and will of God can save him," saying the doctor went inside.

Maggan fell to his knees. He had uncountable money but good wishes. Whom would he ask for good wishes? Rima, Ranjan or the villagers. He had tormented these people all his life and then how would he ask blessings for Sunu?

He prostrated in front of Rima and asked for forgiveness and a little blessing for Sunu.

"Rima, I have come to know everything. Neel had confessed to his crime of involving Sunu and Ranjan to the consumption of drugs. I am genuinely asking for your forgiveness. I would even go to your parents and each and every villager to ask for their forgiveness, but first you must forgive me".

Rima empathized for Maggan. He had blinded himself with money and power and soon he was on the verge of losing his son, for whom he had amassed such wealth. She said, "Whole-hearted penance is the first step to forgiveness. You need to remove the fake label of egotism from your eyes and see the real world. Then the entire world will forgive you."

A doctor came and handed Maggan a prescription. Maggan handed the prescription to an aide and asked the doctor again, "How is Sunu?"

"Just pray. You would need a hundred praying hands for him to survive."

Maggan instructed his driver to start the car. Dhruv and Rima followed him. They went straight to his home. He loaded his car with some trunks and went towards the community pond.

Villagers followed him in astonishment. They had already received the news and were really sad for the young lad. After all, he was a kid from their village no matter how his father was.

Maggan reached the pond, unboxed the trunks and dumped bundles and bundles of currencies into the water. He then took out the stamp papers that he had forged to acquire various lands and the ponds and tore them into pieces. He then turned towards the villagers and asked for their forgiveness.

The villages saw light in his heart and tears in his eyes. They folded their hands and bowed towards the omnipresent for the life of Maggan's son. Soon, they received the news of Sunu being saved by the efforts of doctors and prayers of a hundred hearts.

It is such an irony that throughout his life, Maggan was proud of his behaviour that he was superior to anyone in their village. He was aware of his choices and had a technical cheque list to follow his behaviour. He was formidable to those who seek his consideration and had the zeal for amassing wealth befit for his next seven generations. He was a poor farmer and one day, while ploughing the field, his father stumbled upon a pot of gold coins. The coins were mere plain, solid gold bereft of any insignia of previous kings or kingdom. It was evident that it was hidden there by some unlawful elements years ago. Maggan's father took the pot home and was in a predicament whether he should keep it or hand it over to the government authority. Naturally, greed being the weakest spot, took over his conscience, and he became the richest man in the whole village. Later, Maggan inherited both his property and his nefarious traits as a person. He was so blinded by the love for his wealth and his son that he had turned blind at the transgressions of Sunu, which could even lead to the death of his only son. Maggan lived his whole life in denial, denying himself to taste the nectar of a few good deeds. He was quick to judge and condemn Rima and Ranjan, neglecting his own son's misdeeds. A few decent words or some help in any form could have alleviated him to a noble person, but he chose power and cruelty as the thrill and intoxication of power is greater than drunkenness.

However, this incident had moulded the character of Maggan for the better. There is flexibility in every person and character transformation, though challenging but is possible. People just need will or an incident to change.

Maggan brought back Sunu from the hospital and directly went to meet Rima in the Bank.

"We have no words to thank you or say sorry Rima," Maggan sat on the same chair as he sat on his previous visit.

Rima could notice the difference on his face. His face looked calmer and cheerful, devoid of the wrinkles caused unnecessary by the arrogance he had carried. Three cups of tea were placed by Tarulata in front of them.

"She joined yesterday. She was lucky that the bank had approved her job application." Rima said.

Maggan looked at Tarulata and ask for forgiveness from her too. Tarulata was quick to forgive. Good people don't take a moment to appreciate or forgive. Their hearts are always full of warmth.

"We are taking your leave, Rima. Need to meet so many people to seek forgiveness," Maggan said.

"That would be equivalent to a *char dham yatra*," Rima folded her hands in namaste. Both of them left.

Rima took out her cheque book and wrote legibly in the rupee's row: Two lakhs only. Her heart skipped a beat. He had never withdrawn so much money earlier. It was her entire savings. Nonetheless, her mind was clear and heart devoid of any weight.

In a few minutes, Dhruv came to her desk with her cheque in his hand.

"You will be left with a zero," said an anxious Dhruv.

"I think you haven't heard the phrase that 'money is the grime of hand'. It comes and goes without any notice," Rima said with a smile.

"But it's your entire savings and what is the use of being financially independent if one cannot fulfil her own wishes," Dhruv said in a serious tone.

"But my wishes are not bigger than someone's wish to live pain free. And my dreams would be delayed a little, till I save again. You know I have an earning capacity."

Dhruv was always short of words while arguing with Rima. Dhruv could always help her with money, but would she accept? Dhruv knew the answer. He also knew that he could forever talk with her all his life and fall short of words. He would then stare at her or possibly take her in his arms and feel the warmth of her love. His dream didn't require any money, just love and some courage.

The mud stove was covered in all the soot and cinders. Though Rima had an LPG connection, she often roasted sweet potatoes, brinjals, and other tubers in the mud stove. She loved roasted sweet potatoes and often ate them as a snack with black tea. Padma loved her steamed rice cakes, or a fried rice dumpling with her milk teas. Rima took a damp cloth, cleaned the mud stove, and put some lighted fire sticks from the fireplace. She placed an aluminium kettle filled with water on the stove. It was time for evening tea and Padma wasn't there in the kitchen. She never missed her tea, even on gloomy days. In those days, she would demand tea more often. It calmed Padma's nerves.

Rima took out a steel plate from the wooden cupboard, wiped it clean, and placed two coconut laddoos and a cup of full fat milk tea filled to the brim. She made way to Padma's room. It was a simple room with a twin bed with four vertical wooden columns, one in each corner. The four columns held the strings of a white mosquito net. A dressing table with shaky legs comprised of a rectangular mirror in a wooden frame, a tub of cold cream, a powder with a puff, and a bottle of coconut oil. The room smelt of coconut oil all day. A wide toothed-comb with a few broken teeth, a *tarsel* (tassel of thin fake hair) to make a fake braid and a pain balm for joint pain were the things Rima had seen since day one. Of course, medicines were kept in the kitchen for easy access after meal time. The only things that kept Padma happy were her hand loom work and visits to her sister's house. She usually refrained from mixing too much with the people after her son's death.

Rima saw Padma lying on her bed with the mosquito net on. A mosquito repellent was burning at a corner. She placed the plate on a side table called, "Ma, tea is ready. I have brought it to your room." There was a silence. Padma might have fallen asleep. Rima remembered about the packet kept in her handbag. She rushed to her room and brought the money. She went near Padma, sat on her bed, and touched Padma. Padma tossed and turned to the other side.

Rima could figure out that something was wrong. She unhooked the mosquito net from the pegs and unfolded it. The net acted as a barrier between the two.

"Won't you let me sleep peacefully now," said Padma in an irritating tone.

"The tea would get cold, and you hate cold brews," Rima had her answer ready.

"This is my house, and I can't act according to my will," Padma never let an opportunity go to make Rima feel that.

"I know that well. I just woke you up for your tea and this," Rima handed the money to Padma.

"Ah, by showing money, do you think you have an upper hand in this house? Never and remember it," Padma said.

"Oh, I just gave you this money for your knee operation," Rima told as docilely as she could to suppress a quarrel.

"Where did you get so much money? I think you have taken it from your manager, Dhruv."

"No ma, I have saved enough. Why will I take it from him?"

"I have heard it from people. You both are special friends."

"We are colleagues, but who told you that?"

"Your own mother. I have rented him my house due to my financial problems. You keep your official relations in the office. Don't bring them home", Padma cautioned Rima.

Rima kept the money near Padma and left the room. She was astounded by her mother's behaviour. How could a mother conspire against her own child? Padma was not her own mother, and she could understand her behaviour. She had lost a son who was somehow connected to her life's incident of a single day. But her mother Jyoti had always favoured the ways of the society. Rima got food, shelter, and education from her parents, but they failed to protect her from the hardships of life. They always chose the easier path that provided their daughter with food and a shelter. They had forever ignored her psychological insecurities during her adolescence or the desires of her youth. Could they feel as parents how her life would change marrying a stranger? Nah…it was a usual way of getting married as her mother, Jyoti too married a complete stranger, Hemo, a panchayat clerk. But they felt Rima was lucky to get married to a forest guard who had a permanent job and Rima was working, too. Parents just look after the physical and financial wellbeing and loathed social stigmas. And mental wellbeing…that was what parents ran away from, lest mental wellbeing meant being mad. However, Rima had no qualms about her parents or Padma.

For Padma, Simanta was her entire world. She would accommodate all his wishes, even sometimes outdo her limits. For the forest guard job, she had woven clothes for several nights and days continuously to accumulate the money required as a bribe. Simanta got the job due to her persistent prayers and hard work, so she considered every penny of his salary as her own. Simanta loved her dearly and bought her whatever she required. Padma had spent almost all of her time, energy and money in the pursuits of her son's happiness. In Simanta reflected her proud face, the face of a successful mother.

After Simanta's death, the reflection faded, and it was now Padma's turn to keep the reflection of her son within her. She despised Rima for no fault. Rima was just an entity associated with Simanta and people around them identified as Simanta's mother and widow. Like that, Padma tried to keep the reflection of Simanta shining. Padma gradually got habituated to Rima's care and financial security, but more than that, Padma was insecure. Rima's carefree persona made Padma a little envy. Padma demanded a lot of attention from Rima, which she respectfully obliged.

Padma took the money. There was no necessity to count. She

decided to leave the next day for her sister's home. Her surgery was more important than settling scores with Rima. Rima came to her room and placed a plate of rice, lentils, and pumpkin sabji near her. "I am going to Jaya's house tomorrow. The whole process may take almost two weeks. You take care of the house. I have asked Balen to drop me in the bus stop," saying this Padma touched her plate. Rima went to the kitchen for her dinner.

After dinner, Rima had no mood to take out her project work. She had no money to continue the work at the present time. She folded the washed clothes and placed them in her steel almirah. Her phone beeped. She knew it was Dhruv. She had understood his pulse. She loved talking with him and knew in the whole world it was only Dhruv who understood her. But everything in this world was subjected to conditions, and she hated conditions. Rima's phone beeped.

"Asleep? I can see your lights on,"

"Not yet,"

"I have a surprise for you,"

"What?"

"We are visiting mom next weekend,"

"I don't think I would be able to make it."

"Good night."

Rima smiled. Conditions even here. Why can't things be spontaneous and unconditional?

"Good night. I will try," and she switched off the phone.

Chapter 10

A Familial Dream

It was a three-hour journey from their village to Dibrugarh. Dhruv borrowed a car from Maggan for two days and set on their journey. It was a getaway to get rid of the monotony and recent predicaments that Rima had gone through. The highway was a beautiful stretch of smooth road with trees on both the sides. Soon, they entered the tea territory. On both sides of the road were well grafted tea shrubs. It was early march and the sight of skilful fingers plucking first flush was a sight for sore eyes. 'Flush' denotes the season during which the tea was plucked. In leaf flushing, the leaves on the tea bush are 'flushed'. On the onset of spring when it rained, usually during March, the bushes are flushed with leaves. Leaves plucked during the first flush were the most tender and brewed the best quality of tea.

Dhruv and Rima could feel they were approaching a tea factory as the aroma of roasted tea leaves wafted through the car's window.

"Let us have a tea break. I can't go on ignoring the inviting aroma of the tea," Dhruv suggested.

Both of them got down from the car and went to a roadside tea *dhaba*. "Two plates of paratha and two chai please," Dhruv ordered at the counter and both of them sat on an empty table.

"Are you sure your mom wouldn't mind my presence?" asked an unsure Rima.

"Mind…she would love your presence. Once you meet her, you will know," Dhruv assured her and continued, "Today is her art exhibition and she would meet a lot of people. But I know, when we will meet her, her joy would have no bounds. Who doesn't want to see her child."

Dhruv and Rima entered the District Auditorium. The art gallery was on the first floor. They climbed up the marooned tiled stairs to reach the venue. The room was abuzz with people, news reporters, and VIPs.

"Is your mom a big personality," Rima asked.

"She is my mom and there she is," Dhruv pointed towards a lady.

Nitya Devi was too elegant to be in her fifties. Her butter-coloured complexion perfectly matched with the mauve kurta-pyjama. Her salt and pepper mid length open hair accentuated her beauty. With some kohl and a tinge of nude lipstick, she looked regal. Dhruv opened his arms to hug his mother and dashed towards her like a long-lost kid. Rima had a moment of teary eyes, however she controlled her emotions. For years, the mother son duo had been living apart, yet one could see the contentment on their faces when they met each other. The myriad colours of relations amazed Rima. Maybe her mother too loved her. It's just she wanted to see Rima living a comfortable life.

The room in which Rima was smelt of citrusy, earthy and turpentine. Artworks of various artists had been categorically displayed in an aesthetic way. It was a charity event, so there were no special light or sound effects accentuating the displays. Rima still stood in front of the first painting and watched Nitya showering her motherly affection on Dhruv. After meeting his mother, Dhruv came back to Rima and took her to his mother.

"Ma, this is Rima, my dearest friend and colleague," said Dhruv.

Nitya stared for a few moments in Rima's face and observed her calm face. It was the calmness she had been looking for all her life. Nitya worked wonders with water colours on white canvasses. Mostly, she portrayed the myriad human emotions through her art form. She had mastered the art of portraying rage, depression, loneliness, and happiness to their perfection. 'The Longing of a Child for her Mom' art had earned her a first prize in a major Art Festival. People throng at her art exhibitions to experience a visual euphoria. A range of masterpieces where she had layered emotions on plain canvasses, inducing an enigma on an aesthete, who spent hours in front of her paintings to decipher the layers of emotional perspectives in her art. It was now Nitya's turn to admire God's display of emotions on Rima's face. Nitya would never be able to portray those tranquil eyes and calm face in her paintings. Art came from the fires and desires within us, and Nitya was bereft of that peace within her.

Rima folded her hands in a Namaste, and Nitya embraced her in a warm manner. For a moment, Nitya and the peace came in alignment, and she felt that. She held Rima's hands and walked her through her paintings. Rima was amazed to experience such various dispositions of people in the paintings. And there were paintings of the snow-capped Himalayas, Banaras and many more places that Rima hadn't been to.

"Have you been to all these places?" asked Rima inquisitively.

"Yes Rima, I had been a traveller all my life looking for something in the places that I visit," Nitya gave a complacent reply.

"And have you found that 'something'?"

"Rima, you know, for my painting assignments and my travelling soul, I had been to many countries, wellness retreats, did meditation in the stone-cold Himalayas, attended sessions of distinguished monks and motivational speakers but regretfully, my soul could not find the thing I am looking for. Strange, isn't it?," Nitya gave a concerned look.

"But I am hopeful that you will find your joy. We tend to find our 'the somethings of our life' in the most unusual yet common places. We even don't need to search for it. It would come to us by default as it belongs to us no matter at what stage of life, we find it," Rima said.

"Rima, I have my joy in the form of my son, Dhruv and you are absolutely correct. Whatever is ours will come to us no matter what. I can see a spark of my years long anticipation in none other but in you."

Dhruv was intrigued by the soulful conversations of the two important persons of his life. He would never want to intrude in such an intricate moment. Normally people do not about talk such things in their first meetings, but it was a rare occasion. It was Rima and Nitya.

"Me… Auntie. How could a girl like me merit to harbour your desired expectancies in me?"

"It is all over in your aura. The kind of divine peace you exude. The warmth in your words and the calmness in your face. I had been seeking this positive aura in places, peoples and within self but had failed drastically. I know, it is a persona people are born with but if you seek something passionately, we are bound to receive it, albeit we should be aware it. All my life, I had been chasing an illusion; an illusion named peace. I was not aware how it looked, felt, or behaved. Now that I have seen you, I am sure that peace would find me, no matter where I am," Nitya said.

The Bungalow Tea Resort had a serene atmosphere for exhaling out the tensions and absorb tranquillity. It was more than a customary jaunt with the richness of profound greenery due to the adjoining tea estates. The morning was quite a regular, but Rima's presence turned it into a momentous one. The mist-drenched skies, the charismatic greenery and the mellowed sun could not entice Dhruv, as he was completely engrossed in Rima's aura. Last time, she shared with his mother the room and bits and pieces of his life. He told her about Rima so excitedly that the mother could sense his love for Rima immediately. But Nitya was cautious enough not to make it a family matter, as she knew about boundaries. Those boundaries secured us from unwanted obligations and pressures.

"Rima, Dhruv had told me that you are working on a compendium of wild birds," Nitya asked.

"Yes, sort of. I have sent a sample to a publisher, and they are keen on publishing it but I don't have good quality photographs of the birds, so I am unsure about it. Even if I get a new camera, I wouldn't be able to get hold of pictures of all the birds I already have", Rima sounded a bit dejected.

"Rima, I have worked across major artists of the world. The audience wants to see authenticity, not how expensive the camera is or how recognised a certificate is. All good work is meant for appreciation."

"I know this aunty and I am pursuing this not for some appreciation but following my own callings. I would even like to see a single author copy in my name."

"But if everyone thought like you, we would not have been blessed by the good things in our life. Let alone if God would have thought like you, we would not have the blue skies, green nature, shimmery nights, and kids like you and Dhruv. Isn't it?"

Rima smiled, and Dhruv savoured her smile. How he wished this scene to be a daily affair in their life. He would play the perfect audience to the symphonies of the discussions of the duo. It resonated like sprinkling star dust with the background orchestra and all the good things granted to you in a single shot. Dhruv was clear in his mind that whatsoever, he would always adore these two people his entire life.

Nitya brought her laptop from her room, opened it, and showed some pictures to Rima. Rima was amazed at the preciseness of each creature painted by Nitya. Some paintings were of rare species.

"Do you mind giving me the photographs of the birds that you have shot? I will try my best to give them justice through my art," Nitya proposed.

"I appreciate your generosity, but it would be an irony that a celebrated artist illustrates the scribblings of a newbie writer."

"And you don't know that there are no 'ifs' and 'buts' in art and if there is any, it is business not an art. So I made the proposition. You can mail me the photographs and I will try my best to illustrate them for you."

"How could I thank you even?"

"Just be yourself."

Chapter 11

Uncaging Rima

Rima came home from the office to find Padma sitting at the doorstep. She rushed to open the door, and both went inside. Padma told about her successful surgery and how she had to take some precautions for the rest of her life. In the mid of their conversations, the doorbell rang. It was Rima's parents and brother who had come to visit Padma as a customary visit after medical visits.

Rima went to the kitchen to make tea for all of them. She was surprised at such a usual gathering. Her parents rarely visited. He made milk teas, *puris*, *aloo sabjis*, and *pithas* were always there. The dining table was inundated with good food and decent talks, which was a rarity in their house.

The people provided the support Padma was looking for to speak her mind.

"I have no objection if Rima chooses a life partner for her. Today I am there and tomorrow if I am gone, there would be no one for her. She deserves to have a family life," Padma said in a single breath.

Rima's mother Jyoti burst into tears upon hearing this. All her emotions and guilt had exploded after hearing these words. Jyoti always wanted her daughter's arena to be filled with the basic necessities of life, as all mothers did. Jyoti was not courageous enough to stand for her daughter but wanted a good life for her. When it came from the aggrieving party, she had no issues. Rima's father, Hemo, never had an opinion any day but he too was glad that Rima's mother-in-law had made a wise decision for Rima's future.

Rima was in a state of shock at the words of Padma. It was a new avatar of Padma, like a reincarnation. Padma's voiced had mellowed and her body language had a positive vibe. Rima had her ears for Padma to vent out her remaining sludge.

"The doctor had just operated on me and gave me sedatives to numb the pain of surgery. The sedatives were a bit strong for me, so I went into a deep slumber. I heard numerous voices, of doctors and nurses, other patients and then of my parents and my fellow people. I could not decipher what each of one was saying. But one voice was distinct. 'Ma, who will look after Rima when you come to my abode to look after me? She is a pure girl. She had sacrificed all her savings just for you even after you are ever ready to humiliate her'. It was Simanta's voice. I could differentiate it among a thousand others. I felt a sharp pain in my chest and woke up with a start. He was not there, but I have to fulfil every wish of his like I had always done," saying this, Padma had tears in her eyes.

"Look Rima, I am an old soul who has no future. Jaya is all alone now, and she has been pestering me to stay with her. Tell me if you have someone in your mind. I will talk to his parents," said Padma.

"Rima, you are lucky to have Padma as your mother-in-law. Who thinks of getting her daughter-in-law married to some another person? Grasp the opportunity and, if required, your father and I are also open to initiate discussion for your remarriage. Do you have Dhruv in your mind?" asked Jyoti.

Rima paused and looked at her people. Is her life a mere jump from one bondage to another? Would she always be patented as someone's daughter, wife, daughter-in-law, or maybe mother? She respected relations and had never fussed upon carrying out her responsibilities diligently, but imposing a relation for the sake of having a partner was out of her comprehension. All her childhood, she had played a second fiddle to her brother. The incident with Simanta was merely an accident where she was not given any scope for explanation. She had absolutely no role in Simanta's death however, she was branded as an ill-fated woman. She had been looking after a woman who had never had a decent word for her. In her heart she knew she loved Dhruv immensely, but she was not prepared for this step, and she was even not sure if Dhruv had the same feelings for her.

Rima voiced slowly yet firmly, "I am more than happy to receive your love and affection, but to be honest, I don't want to be entangled in a marital relationship so soon. It is not that my priorities are bigger than my relationships or my belief in marriage has been forsaken, but I want to live for some days without any societal ties or bondages, be it in a cage or in an open forest."

Her mother wanted to say a word, but Padma restrained her. "I know her. Let her be herself."

Chapter 12

Love Forever

Dhruv was astonished to receive the transfer order. So soon. He had to leave for Guwahati the next day. Though he loved Rima with all his soul, he had never got a chance to convey his feelings to her, or maybe he was a little scared lest he might lose her forever. But today he made up his mind to open his heart in front of her.

Rima, too, got the news of his transfer. Her eyes were moist, and her heart carried a heaviness since the time she had got the news. She didn't leave her seat once or had talked to Dhruv. Her phone beeped. She knew it was Dhruv.

Meet me in the backyard tonight.

Tears rolled down her cheeks.

Dhruv and Rima sat on a bench in the backyard of their house. Their hearts were brimming with emotions, but lips dry. Dhruv, with a little courage, held her hand. She was in tears and sank into his arms. They hugged each other as if they were statues from eternity.

"I love you, Rima."

"I love you too Dhruv."

"Are you coming with me?"

"What do you want?"

"I want Rima to be herself. I shall wait for you forever."

"We are for each other. For eternity,"

And they hugged again.

Sometimes, to be in love is to be attached forever till love slowly vaporises like a camphor in mysterious silence and the emotional bond between the two beings in love gradually detaches from each other due to lack of the unconditional love or excess of familial and social obligations. Lovers become responsible family beings looking upon the utmost need that can be fulfilled by time, money, or other worldly things. Just as the essence of camphor lingers on for a while, the fragrance of love drives the two people till normal death do them apart. Till death, possessiveness is one of the key factors of love (read familial love) but as we die, possessiveness dies, ownership dies and the in evidently "I can do anything for your love" dies too.

Dhruv and Rima had never got the love they wanted till they met each other. They came of their shells to realize love for each other, pervading societal norms and emotional barriers. And so much for not naming their relationship with a worthy secured name in the name of impressing the society or holding the possession of each other's individuality. Dhruv and Rima always laughed about the concepts of soulmates or souls after life and termed them as poetic perceptions or fictional phrases. They believed in their one life, and they believed in each other, but most importantly, they believed in that one moment that defined love for both of them. Rima always said that "We are born for that one special moment and the rest of our lives, we prepare ourselves to encounter that moment and savour it for the rest of our lives."

Dhruv and Rima had diverse dreams but the same beliefs. They had different desires, but the same destination. They had separate journeys but the same stoppages. They were different, but they were one.

Rachita Baruah is a banker and loves to scribble musings and poems when she is not reading books. Her micro tales have been selected and featured in Pocketful O' stories, Mithaas, etc. She has also won the Harper Collins Summer Reads Micro fiction contest. She has written poems for radio and newspapers earlier, and her short stories have been featured in several anthologies. 'When Life Teaches' is a collection of short poems that has been self-published on Amazon Kindle.

INKFEATHERS
PUBLISHING

www.inkfeathers.com

We love creating beautiful books for you!

Be a part of our ever-growing community of authors.
Grow, write, and publish with us!

Connect with us on socials.
We'd love to hear from you!

@InkfeathersPublishing

Made in United States
Orlando, FL
22 October 2024

53000913R00050